ED AND ME

ED AND ME

Written and illustrated by
DAVID McPHAIL

Harcourt Brace Jovanovich, Publishers
San Diego   New York   London

Library of Congress Cataloging-in-Publication Data
McPhail, David M.
Ed and me.
Summary: A small girl and her father buy an old
pickup truck named Ed, and build a garage
to store it in.
[1. Trucks — Fiction] I. Title.
PZ7.M478818Ed   1990   [E]   86-3175
ISBN 0-15-224888-9

First edition   A B C D E

The paintings in this book were done in watercolor with linework drawn
in black ink on 140-lb. Fabriano hot-press paper.
The display type was set in Adroit Medium.
The text type was set in Cloister.
Composition by Thompson Type, San Diego, California
Color separations were made by Bright Arts, Ltd., Hong Kong.
Printed and bound by Tien Wah Press, Singapore
Production supervision by Warren Wallerstein and Ginger Boyer
Designed by Trina Stahl

For Jaime

When I first met Ed, he belonged to my father's friend
D'Neal . . . and to D'Neal's friend, Rugby.

Rugby loved to go for rides in Ed and could often be seen
with his head hanging out the window, ears flapping in the
breeze.

"If you ever decide to sell Ed," my father told D'Neal,
"please let me know."

    It was later that year, around Christmastime, that Ed came to live with us.

    "Poor Ed looks lost and empty without Rugby," my father said to D'Neal. "Are you sure you won't include Rugby in the bargain?"

    "Not a chance," said D'Neal, laughing. "Not a chance at all!"

We didn't use Ed right away. He just sat out there in the
yard all winter, collecting snow and ice, and looking very
lonesome.

But when spring came, Ed was raring to go.

My father got in, turned the key, and good old Ed sprang to life.

"Amazing!" said my father.

After that we used Ed nearly every day.

We went to the post office to get the mail (and sometimes an ice-cream cone next door at the village store).

In haying season Ed carried hay back to the barn to be put up for the horses' winter food.

Ed carried us down to the lake . . .

and waited patiently while we had a swim.

We went on picnics with Ed . . .

and decorated him for the Fourth of July parade.

One night I even pitched a tent in the back of Ed and camped out. I didn't stay *all* night, though. Just until my flashlight batteries ran out.

When it came time to bring in the firewood from the forest, Ed was all heart. But we took small loads and made many trips.

"No sense in breaking Ed's back," said my father.

Every once in a while Ed took sick and needed the careful
attention of Dennis and Ken at the gas station.

My father says that when you get to be Ed's age you have
to start taking things easy. My father is even older than Ed.

In autumn we carried apples, squashes, pumpkins, and the rest of the harvest in Ed.

Then the nights started getting cold. Winter was coming back.

"Is Ed going to have to stay outside again this winter?" I asked my father.

"I hadn't much thought about it," my father replied.

"I think he would like it better inside," I said.

"And I think you're right!" said my father.

So we used Ed for one more thing before winter arrived.

We went to the sawmill and bought a load of lumber. And
with that lumber we built a small barn — just for Ed!

When it was finished, my father backed Ed inside.

"He looks snug and cozy to me," said my father. And as we stood looking at Ed in his new home, the first snowflake landed gently on my nose.

"He looks happy, too," I said. "Just like me."